# MARRYING THE PROTECTIVE PROFESSOR

IRIS WEST

To my readers. I hope you love Blossom Ford, and the sexy men, curvy women and kind but extremely interfering folk that live there, as much as I do.

# 1 AUGUST

ALL MY LIFE I've secretly wished I was born and raised in an ordinary family, with loving, welcoming parents instead of being the town's sign of bad luck, growing up at Blossom Ford Orphanage and having the town's name as my surname, like the other kids there. I can't help believing if I was wanted, the acceptance and sense of belonging would have helped me become someone who knows how to love. That belief is strongest when I think of Ella Mitchell.

It's Friday night so ensuring she gets home safely is my top priority as I park my SUV a short distance from Jackson's Diner where she's working, far enough to see the door of the restaurant but not so close that anyone might link my presence to the diner. I don't care how the interfering residents of Blossom Ford view me, but I don't want rumors to spread about Ella.

I slide down the car seat, getting comfortable even

as I curse myself for the warmth that spreads through my chest at the mere thought of her name. As I've done a millionth time, I tell myself I'm here to protect her.

An uncomfortable tightness in my chest and a bitter taste in my mouth that I'm all too familiar with have me exhaling slowly. But it's hard to chase away the guilt. I cannot keep from committing the same sin. I'm a scarred, divorced, grizzly mountain of a man that's old enough to be her father while she's a beautiful, innocent twenty-two-year-old with her whole life ahead of her. Ella deserves better than me. But I still can't stop thinking about her.

It makes no difference that what I feel for her is more than physical attraction. I love her strength, soft smile and the way she's warm to everyone that crosses paths with her. There's a certainty in my bones that she's meant for me alone. This only makes the guilt worse. I should let her go because I love her.

And I have. To a point. For the last two years since I returned to Blossom Ford, saw her for the first time and fell for the kindness in her honey hued eyes and the sweetest curves I'd ever seen, I've stopped myself from approaching her. From claiming her. At least in real life. Because in my dreams, I've made love to her every single night and spent my days laughing with her. I've always considered my self-control one of my strongest attributes, but I can't stop dreaming about her.

I can't help the fact that I won't have her driving home by herself at midnight, after her shifts at the diner on Fridays and Saturdays. If I'm an asshole, so be it. And if deep down I know as well as ensuring she's safe, I have to see her face, I'll take the guilt and deal with it.

I frown when only two cars remain in the parking lot. One is old Jackson's beat up truck, and the other belongs to Rosie; the woman who works with Ella. Ella's old yellow mini should be right besides Rosie's.

The door to the diner flies open and Rosie marches out in her apron, phone glued to her ear. She sprints to her car. My frown thickens. How is Ella going to get home? Will she be closing on her own? I force myself to stay in the car. As much as I want to rush in and help, keeping a distance is crucial to my self-discipline.

I ramp up the air conditioning in the car a little higher. It usually takes one hour to close, but tonight, it'll take Ella longer. Old Jackson doesn't think hard work hurts women. There's no way he's going to help with setting the dinner to the way he likes it.

I keep my eyes on the door and an hour and a half later, I'm rewarded with the sight of Ella's curvy hips wrapped in hugging denim and the soft way her breasts hug her blouse. Even after a ten-hour shift, she's a vision that gets my heart racing.

She zeroes in on my car and it's like she can see me, like she knows I'm waiting here for her. She does this on Fridays and Saturdays; the days I wait for her. If she worked any other nights, I'd wait for her then, too. She's friends with Mrs. Gallagher, the orphanage director who's the closest thing to a mother I've ever had. Ella must think of me as a much older brother who's looking out for her.

She steps on the street and heads towards me. I know that she's just taking the road to her house, but I can't stop my heart from beating even faster. It's like this every time I see her.

I'm feeling something else too; anger. Her walking alone down the empty street at this time of the night is pissing me off.

She's only a few feet from me when a car careens down the street and stops beside her. I sit up straight, hoping a friend is coming to pick her up. But she doesn't slow down, even after spotting the car.

I scowl as a man stumbles out of the car and steps in her path. It's Toby Anderson, Ella's ex. Something ugly rears in me. Despite my unstoppable feelings for Ella, whenever I see him, I realize how great my self-control is. Every time I saw him with Ella, I wanted to knock him out. The four months they dated were an exercise in self-discipline I didn't think I was going to win. But for Ella, to give her the chance at happiness she deserved with someone her age that could give her a comfortable life, I held myself back.

I don't like the way Toby sways on his feet. The light from the full moon and lamppost in front of the diner are enough to make out the disgust on Ella's face. Before I know it, my hand is on the door handle, but my eyes don't stray from Toby.

They are talking but the loud music and shouts from

the car stop me from hearing what they are saying. Toby reaches out a hand and touches Ella's arm. She wrenches it back.

I'm out of the car. I sprint towards them, her safety the only thought in my mind. For her, I'd tried staying away, but her safety is something I'll not compromise on. Even if it means she might hate me for interfering with her life.

# 2 ELLA

"STAY AWAY FROM me!" I move back, keeping my eyes on Toby's face even as my hand reaches for the pepper spray inside my bag. The expression in Toby's eyes is creeping me out.

"Bitch," he spits and takes a step toward me.

My hand reaches for the spray, but before I can whisk it out, Toby's hand reaches towards me so fast I close my eyes.

A grunt and surprised shouts reach my ears. When I inch my eyes open, the first thing I see is August Ford, crushing back Toby's arm. The younger man struggles to pull away, but he doesn't stand a chance against August's toned muscles.

Relief floods through me.

"Who the fuck are you?" Toby screams.

"I believe the lady doesn't want to speak with you. I'll let you go if you are ready to get back into your car and drive off."

Toby's face is twisted in pain. One of his friends comes out of the car. And cowers back in when August's eyes arrow in on him.

I'm glad Toby's friends won't gang up against August, who shoves Toby towards his car. Toby stumbles before righting himself. The venom in his eyes as he glares at me has my stomach tightening in knots.

"We're not done."

August stands beside me and puts his arm around my shoulders, pulling me close so that my side is flush against his. I blink up at him, but his eyes are arrowed in on Toby.

"I believe you are. If I see you sniffing around my woman again, it won't end with an armlock." There's a menace in his quiet voice that might have sent chills down my spine had his arm not been cradling me.

Toby's eyes widen, wariness replacing the bravado. He takes in August's arm around my shoulder. I embrace August and gaze at him adoringly, which doesn't require much acting on my part.

Toby looks at me and the expression that made me finally muster up the courage to break up with him is back in his face. August moves in front of me and takes a step towards Toby. With an angry shout, the younger man finally gets into his car and drives off, tyres screeching.

"Are you okay?" August asks?

"Thank you, Mr. Ford." That's what I call him when he comes to the diner and the odd time I've bumped into him at the orphanage.

August winces, making me wonder what upset him. I've been calling him August in my mind and Mr. August when I'm with other people for so long that I'm not at all worried I'll make a mistake in front of him.

"I'll take you home."

The polite thing would be to refuse, to say I don't want to put him out of his way but I'm finally getting a chance to sit close to the man that's haunted my dreams for the last two years so I'm not going to be coy about it.

We make the brief journey to his car in silence. I thank him as he opens the passenger door, then watch his long legs stalk across the front of the car. Not only do I love his deep-set gray eyes, the graying hair at his temples and his enormous size that makes me feel safe, I also find the way he walks hot. I should think about that icy expression in Toby's eyes just before he left and wonder how I am going to deal with him but being this close to August is making me remember all the times I've spotted his car as I drive home on Fridays and Saturdays nights.

At first, before I realized it was him, I was worried. But when I found out the car belonged to him, for the first time since I began working at Jackson's Diner, I started looking forward to Fridays and Saturdays for another reason other than tips. Then I dared to hope.

Hope that he'd fall for me and ask me out.

But six months later, I gave up. August Ford was an experienced man. If he wanted a woman, he didn't have to take such a roundabout way to ask her out. So I came up with another theory. He wanted to make sure I was safe. It wasn't such a farfetched idea. He grew up at the orphanage, so it was possible he wanted to protect me because I was friends with Mrs. Gallagher and an orphan myself.

Whatever the reason, I decided to view him as my guardian angel.

I glance at his muscular hands on the steering wheel, fascinated by the casual way he handles the powerful car. It reminds me of where those skillful hands have been in my dreams, and a curl of desire flickers in my belly. When he looks at me, I turn away, feeling heat creep up my neck and face.

"Why are you walking home alone at this time of the night?"

His voice is thick like dark molasses and there's anger in it. I face him. Is he mad he got involved?

"My car broke down. I was going to get a lift with Rosie, but she had an emergency and left early."

"Call a cab next time."

I don't like the command in his voice, but I remind myself he just saved me from what could have turned into a dangerous situation. Toby was sweet when he was sober. That's why I went out with him in the first place, but when he drank, a mean streak took hold of him.

"I did, but they were giving me an hour's estimated time of arrival and I was too tired to wait that long." I should really have booked a cab as soon as Rosie left, but I was rushed off my feet and didn't have time to do it.

A grunt. He stops at a red light and looks at me. "I'll give you my number. Call me if you can't get a ride after work."

I'm not sure how to respond to that, so I just stare at him.

"If Mrs. Gallagher finds out I knew you were in danger but did nothing to help, she'll pull my ears until they are red. I'm just protecting myself." His lips curve.

I've never seen him smile before. He looks younger, playful even, and that makes him more attractive. I can feel my answering smile.

"I can't imagine Mrs. Gallagher pulling your ears."

"That's because you didn't know her when she was younger. She's softened with age."

The light turns green; he pulls away. "You still haven't given me an answer."

"Okay." I glance around the luxurious car, wishing my house were further away and not a five-minute car ride.

As soon as the vehicle stops, I open the door. August is already being kind to me. I don't want to take up any more of his time.

He gets out of the car and strides round to me.

"I'll walk you to your front door," he says, looking around the low-rise apartment block.

I take the stairs to the second floor, glad that I live in a relatively fine area of Blossom Ford. When I'm in front of my door, I turn to face him. I want to offer him at least a coffee, but am not sure how he'll respond to that.

"I'd like to discuss something with you. Do you have time Sunday?"

It's my only day off. I nod, wondering what is on his mind. "What time?"

He waits as I close the door after we agree on a time and place to meet. I stand with my back against it, listening to his footsteps fade as he walks back down the stairs. Sighing, I throw my bag on the sofa, head to the bathroom, and shower. I can't stop thinking about those hands as he masterfully handled the car and the safe way they made me feel when he embraced me.

As hot water pounds against my skin, my hand glides between my breasts, belly and circles my clit. Pleasure surges as I tip my head back and continue stroking, eyes closed. When I replay August saying I'm his woman in that rough voice of his, I moan and circle faster. I imagine his strong fingers taking over mine, his long middle finger sliding inside me and I come apart with a cry.

Switching off the shower, I shake my head. The nights I sense August following me, I usually stroke myself to sleep. I was too excited to make it to bed tonight.

# 3 AUGUST

I WISH I was drinking a double whisky as Ella enters the new coffee shop in town. A burned orange dress hugs her soft brown curves and impossibly high heel sandals cover her feet. I'm not the only one staring. A couple of other men are staring at her, too. She is so beautiful that she turns heads wherever she goes. But I've been near her long enough to know she doesn't even realize the chaos she leaves in her wake.

I stand up and immediately she spots me. A smile that reaches her eyes and makes them crinkle splits her face. And I question what I'm about to do. There's trust in her gaze that no doubt comes from believing Mrs. Gallagher asked me to keep an eye on her. But then I remember Toby's behavior and the doubt slips away.

Once we're both settled with steaming cups of coffee, she looks at me with her large, honey eyes and I know I'll do anything to protect her.

"Have you thought about what you'll do if Toby approaches you again? If I hadn't been there, he would have hit you."

Ella sips her drink, but I don't miss the way her eyes narrow before she looks down at her cup. Having to pack in college after only her first year, burying her parents and taking guardianship of her thirteen-year-old sister all on her own made her independent and self-reliant. She doesn't like it when people try to give her charity. As well as getting involved in her business, I'm being bossy.

I'm trying to be as gentle as I can, but it seems that's something I can't do. It's what Lily, my ex-wife, said when we divorced; that I'm too domineering. But even though I know there's a danger it'll alienate Ella, her safety matters too much for me not to go ahead with my plan.

"You gave him a good scare; I doubt he'll come back."

Something about the way she speaks has my instincts rearing up.

"It's not the first time he's done this since you broke up, is it?"

Ella shrugs. "If he comes back, I'll sort it out."

"How?"

Ella takes another sip of her drink.

"I have a solution that will benefit us both," I say.

Ella stares at me. "I can handle it."

"Hear me out. We can help each other."

Ella leans forward, searching my face. Her willingness to help others frustrates me yet today it might work in my favor.

"I've been thinking of getting a housekeeper. I'm set in my ways and housekeepers I've had in the past haven't been a good fit because of that. If you're willing to help, the job comes with accommodation - for you and your sister when she's on break from school, holiday pay and flexible hours. Mrs. Gallagher mentioned a while back you wanted to go back to college to finish your degree. This could be a good way of doing it. Especially now Blossom Ford has a college. You don't have to go far or you could study online."

I pause. I can almost hear Ella's thoughts; she's interested but suspicious too. I tried to keep the salary low, it's only twice what she's earning now.

I have to up the game, even though what I'm about to tell her is embarrassing to admit. Especially in front of her.

"I live alone. During term time, I'm so busy I don't notice the time passing. But summer breaks, it gets lonely. I'd be glad to have company during dinner, rather than eating alone every day." This is the hardest thing I've had to talk about since my divorce. I'm fucking blushing the way I did when I was fifteen and asked my first crush out on a date.

I gulp my coffee and force myself to peer at Ella.

Compassion is stamped across her face and frustration rears its ugly head again even though I'm happy she's reacted this way.

"You're on your own because you want to be. All the single women of Blossom Ford would kill for a date with you. You only need to smile at them."

"What about you?" I can't resist teasing her.

She looks at her coffee. When she finally looks up, there's a huge smile on her face. "I'm just like all the other women. But you're way out of my league." She skims the side of the cup with her index finger.

I'm the one who's out of her league. But I nod. "For this to work well, we should get a marriage of convenience."

Ella chokes on her coffee. I pass her some tissues.

"Sorry," she says when her coughing fit passes. "I was just so surprised."

I wait for her to elaborate.

"You don't have to go that far to help me," she says.

"We're helping each other. We'd have a contract; you can cancel it anytime you want. Marriage carries more weight than a boyfriend/girlfriend relationship. Toby won't bother you if he knows you're married to me and I'll have company in the evenings and a housekeeper who's likely to be more tolerant of me because I'm friends with her friend. When your life changes, you're free to leave. I'm not planning on getting married again, but if things change for me, I'd still need a housekeeper. It's a win-win situation for both of us." The only woman I'd ever want to be married to is Ella, but I keep my voice light.

"Can I think about it? I'd have to leave the diner; I've been there for four years. It's a big decision."

"I only have a few weeks before term starts, it'd be nice to have company before I go back to work. I'm sure the registry office could fit us in with a couple of days' notice." This is better than saying everyday she's living alone there's a chance that dork Toby might harass her.

# 4 ELLA

"YOU MAY KISS the bride," the Registry Officer says.

My heart pounds harder than a few minutes ago when I said I do. It doesn't seem to matter that this marriage isn't real. Standing in front of August in this white dress is making my heart believe it's real.

There's an expression in his eyes that I can't decipher. He looks into my eyes. His hands reach for the back of my neck. A zing of electricity makes my nerve endings stand to attention. Then his thumbs stroke my cheeks and my breath hitches. I'm frozen, my eyes caught in his, as they slowly snake towards me.

The moment I sense his breath, my eyes close. His lips are soft against mine, a light caress, but they touch the deepest part of me. I've been dreaming of this moment for eons. As if being controlled by a puppet master, I open my lips. He sighs and then his tongue is inside mine.

Wanting to be closer to him, I stand on my tiptoes and wrap my arms around his neck. I tilt my head to give him better access. His tongue inside mine is everything I've dreamed of. In just a few moments August will-

A cough reaches my foggy brain. August lets go of my cheeks and places his arms around my shoulders. I bite my lip as I realize where we are and who's around us. I'm so grateful for August's hands, which stop me from sliding to the floor; my knees are so weak.

Telling myself to get over my still raging hormones and the embarrassment on my cheeks, I nod. August's hands fall away from me. I copy him as he turns towards the Registry Officer. She smiles as she tells us we can go.

A cheering sound booms from behind us and I turn around to see my best friend Winona still whooping and Mrs. Gallagher clapping her hands, her cheeks moist. A piercing arrow of sadness hits my heart and I blink back tears. Would Mum have been crying right now, like Mrs. Gallagher? I shake my head. I've been thinking about Mum and Dad while making my decision, choosing this dress August insisted on paying for, getting dressed and walking down the aisle.

When we are outside, Mrs. Gallagher and Winona insist on taking pictures on the vivid greenery of Blossom Ford's Registry office. It's a beautiful day; the sun is shining so strongly, as if to wish us well and make the most of the last few weeks of summer as Winona said, when she was helping me get dressed earlier.

We go to Luigi's for a light meal. It's the classiest restaurant in Blossom Ford. I'd protested against going there, but August said we needed to make sure everyone knew we were married, so there'd be no doubt in Toby's mind about our relationship.

I manage only a few bites and drink a few too many glasses of champagne. When I hug Winona and Mrs. Gallagher goodbye, I can't help shedding a few tears. They are both so hopeful this marriage will work - their optimism touches that deepest recess of my mind wishing for the same thing, even though I should know better.

Mrs. Gallagher knows nothing about the truth of our marriage. I totally agree with August that it'll upset her to know Toby was bothering me. But Winona knows. I had to tell someone, needed someone to sound my ideas on. I should have known that Winona would totally be for this marriage. Since she caught me staring at August one day when he was at the diner last winter, she's known about my crush on him.

I was only glad I'd managed to keep it to myself for a year. Winona had a sixth sense when it came to relationships. She didn't want to admit it, but she was just as good as her mother wend female ancestors who run Blossom Ford's ancient, successful matchmaking agency.

"Once you live with him, August will have no hope against your beauty. I've told you a million times that he fancies you. Trust me," she'd said in my apartment the evening August proposed. I'd been too scared to go to her house in case her mother or grandmother heard our conversation.

We are both silent as August drives us home. I can't believe I'm already thinking of his house as home. It's only been four days since he proposed. I bite my lip as my sister Susie pops into my mind. After hours of agonizing over what to do, I decided not to tell her I was getting hitched. She's volunteering her medical services in Tanzania during summer break and she's worked so hard to pay for the trip, I didn't have the heart to ask her to come back. Besides, I don't know how things are going to work out with August. It's better not to worry her. She's going straight to Brooklyn when summer break is over. There'll be plenty of time to tell her. I did, however, tell her I rented the apartment and was working as a living in housekeeper for Mr. Ford.

We drive into August's mansion (it's hard to describe it as anything else) and I look around. I'd always wondered what the houses on this side of Blossom Ford looked like inside, after admiring the green lawns outside and large glass windows. I'd always believed it must be bright inside during the summer, with all the sunlight going inside. August's grass is much taller than that of the other houses and his garden isn't as neat, a fact I've overheard many customers at the diner complain about.

When we arrive in front of the front door, he tells me to wait inside. I watch as he moves round to my side and opens the door. A thrill runs through me. I doubt I'll get used to this anytime soon.

I wait for him to walk to the front door so I can follow, but he reaches out and lifts me. I'm so startled, my arms go round him to steady myself.

August laughs. It's a deep sound that goes so well with his voice, but it's innocent too, and my lips tug up.

"We may as well follow tradition, just in case any of my noisy neighbors are watching."

I nod, still shocked at the boyish look on his face. The house stands on its own and the nearest houses are a little farther away, but I know very well one can never be too careful in Blossom Ford.

"My right trouser pocket," August says when we reach the door.

It's a little awkward to get round to his pocket. My hand slides over his muscular thigh and I mumble a sorry before I insert my hand correctly. Triumphantly, I hold the key and look up at him, but he's no longer laughing. Smoldering gray eyes stare down at me, unbridled desire darkening their usual light tone.

My breath catches. But before I can do anything, August's lids slide down and when he looks back up, that burning gaze is gone.

"Can you manage?" he asks lightly.

As I grapple with the door and finally open it, I

wonder if I imagined that stare of naked desire.

As soon as we're over the threshold, August puts me down. He shows me around the large kitchen, reception rooms, study, as well as the rooms upstairs. When we reach his room, I stare around the massive bed and furniture. But, apart from a photo of Mrs. Gallagher with her husband and one of August with Mrs. Gallagher in the study, there aren't any other pictures. My heart wrenches. This is a beautiful house. Why does it look like there's not much life inside it?

# 5 AUGUST

AS I PULL out the few pans in the kitchen drawers, flashes of the wedding night of my first marriage go through my mind. I wince at the hope I had then. I believed Lily and I were so in love we'd grow old together. I wanted to spend all my free time with her and showered her with what I thought was affection. Lily called it being clingy. I will not make the mistakes I made with her again. I'm going to give Ella space, even if all I want to do is spend as much time with her as possible. Footsteps sound by the door and I turn towards them.

Ella's wearing a baby blue track suit and fluffy black slippers. I've never seen her looking so cute and soft. Warmth spreads through me. I want to see her every day like this. I'm not sure if it's because she's not wearing make-up or the fact we're in our indoor clothes, but there's a sense of intimacy in the kitchen.

"Sorry I'm late; I dozed off."

There's a tentative air about her, like she's not sure how she'll be welcomed. As if she's decided, she tucks her sleek, shoulder-length, black hair behind her ears and comes to examine the pots.

"Is this all you've got?" she asks.

I smile, hoping it'll relax her.

"I can use these two. Do you have pasta?"

I nod and head towards a cupboard. She goes to the fridge, rummages there and returns with lettuce and tomatoes.

"Pasta and tomato sauce with salad it is. I'll go grocery shopping tomorrow."

"We'll go together. Remember the companionship side of our agreement? Also, it'll be beneficial to be seen around town."

Ella's eyes are enormous, but she nods.

"My cooking repertoire consists of grilled cheese and peanut butter sandwiches. So, tell me what to do."

Ella laughs and shakes her head. More warmth spreads through me. I stand beside her as we prepare the food, my part mostly cutting ingredients. I've seen her laugh at the diner and orphanage, but knowing she's laughing because of me has me wrapped up in knots.

"How did you learn to cook?" I ask as she stirs onions in olive oil, totally absorbed in what she's doing.

After a couple of heartbeats, she looks up. "My mum taught me. She'd wait until Dad got home and washed up, then she'd order us to cut and wash vegetables and bring anything she needed. Susie and I were also the tasters." There's a smile in her voice, but I can also hear sadness.

"Would you rather not talk about them?"

Ella shakes her head and her jet-black hair sways on her shoulders. "Talking about them helps to keep their memory alive." She stops and grins.

"What is it?"

"Flour."

"What?" I ask, a little confused but enthralled by the mischievous look that transforms her expression.

"Dad once spilled a bag of flour while opening it. It went all over his clothes. I must have been about eight at the time and the sight of his immense body, hair and beard covered in fluffy white flour was too much for me. I burst out laughing. Dad tried to take revenge, and a war broke out. After that, Mum insisted we wore our oldest clothes whenever we were making pastry."

"Sounds like you had fun cooking with your family." I would love to have that with her; to cook and play with Ella and our kids.

"Put the carrots in," Ella watches as I carefully slide the grated orange bits into the pan. She holds out the spoon.

I grab it and stir.

"There's a rota for chores at the orphanage. I would have thought you'd be a decent cook."

"Cook and I didn't get along. Since kitchen duty

was the only chore that ended with a treat, I always avoided her by swapping with one of the other kids." When I was little, I didn't understand why Cook treated me differently from the other kids. It only made sense after I started school and learned why the other kids called me a sign of bad luck. "I guess you can teach me," I change the subject.

There's compassion in Ella's eyes. Some of the old folks in town still walk the other way when they see me so she probably knows my story. She looks like she's going to say more, but then she turns to the stove and says, "Add a little water."

She stands there looking at me, making me feel like a pupil. "What were you studying at college?" I ask because the notion of Ella watching me is turning me on.

"Finance." She checks the pasta and grabs a kitchen towel. "I didn't know what I wanted to do, but I was good with numbers, so I chose that. It's only now I've volunteered at the orphanage that I've learned running a place like that is what I'd like to do."

"Mrs. Gallagher would hire you straight away."

"Did you always want to be a professor?" Ella asks.

"No. I love studying living organisms, so I was a researcher for years before one of my professors asked me to cover him for a few months. I loved it and now I do both."

As we cook and eat, we talk about my work and Ella's family's amusing kitchen antics. The sun is setting by the time we finish. When Ella asks if I'd like to sit outside and watch the golden rays descend on the horizon, I lead the way, taking the bottle of wine we started drinking.

We sit mostly in silence. After our time in the kitchen, the quiet is comfortable, as if two good friends are sitting side by side. I realize the last time I watched the sun set was the day I graduated high school and left Blossom Ford. Before that, I used to sneak out of the orphanage to watch the sunset at Blossom Ford Point.

Weekends, the place was busy with groups of young people hanging out, but during most weekdays, there was only the murmur of the river - and in the spring the cherry blossom petals falling on the ford - to keep me company. The solitude was bliss after the chaos of the orphanage.

"It's late. I should go to bed." There's a reluctance in Ella's voice that's egging me to ask her to stay longer. I tamp down on the urge, reminding myself she's here so I can keep her safe.

"Goodnight." My voice betrays nothing of the need to hold her, kiss those strawberry lips and have Ella's body flush against mine.

***

## Ella

AUGUST AND I are visiting the orphanage. I volunteer a couple of days a month, helping with cooking, mending clothes and linen, but I didn't know August also volunteered. So far, he's taken care of odd jobs inside the main building as well as mowed the lawn.

I have never been this kind of happy before. Cooking and eating all my meals with August and sitting in the garden in the evenings with him, drinking wine and talking brings me a contentment I never thought I'd have with him.

I've also never been this kind of frustrated before. The day of the wedding, I know I didn't mistake the red-hot embers in August's eyes when we kissed at the church and before he carried me into the house. Even if I had, almost every day I catch him looking at me, the desire in his eyes so raw, I know he wants me as much as I want him.

But he does nothing about it. Toby was my first boyfriend and since we only lasted four months, I have little experience with men, but I've tried everything I know to seduce him short of walking out naked in front of him. Shorts that are almost indecent and off the shoulder tops darken his gaze and make him steal more glances of me, but they don't make him touch me.

For the last two weeks, I've been alternating between bliss and frustration. And it's getting harder not to show. Something else bothers me. I've shared so much with August but I can't help feeling he's keeping a distance from me. Sure, I'm normally a chatty person, but I don't share my personal life with everyone. August makes me want to share. And I like the way talking about my family and dreams seems to make him happy. I like that he's smiling more and more.

I'm carrying a basket of linen when I spot August in the small room Mrs. Gallagher keeps for any of the kids that want a quiet place to study. He's tutoring a sixteen-year-old who's graduating from high school next year. I shake my head at the hero worship going on. Just like August, Leo wants to be a biologist.

August is saying something I can't hear, but his expression has me catching my breath. He's engrossed. His total focus is on making sure Leo understands whatever he's tutoring. My heart skips a beat and in that moment, I realize I've fallen in love with August Ford. I'm helplessly in love with the way he looks at me like I'm the only woman in the world.

As if he's aware someone is watching him, he looks towards me. I bolt. I can't pretend I'm not affected by him. The laundry room is empty, I take refuge in it.

When I was young, I'd always fantasized about falling in love. It was going to be a wonderful moment. However, worry fills me as I pick up a sheet, find a tear and begin mending. August's guardedness and refusal to touch me makes me worry that although he might fancy me, deep down he really views me as a very young friend of someone he loves rather than the woman I want him to see me as. It's alright for him to help me, but I'm starting to feel like he doesn't believe I can cope with the deepest worries of his life.

# 6 AUGUST

AS SOON AS I wake up, I'm down. This day has come round too quickly. A wave of sorrow and desolation pull me into the deepest abyss and I remember what day it is. August the thirty-first. Usually, a couple of days before, I'll know it's coming. For the first time since I realized Mrs. Gallagher's husband, Kenzie Gallagher, died on this day trying to save me and my mother, who jumped into the river, I didn't go through the usual warning period.

It's because of Ella. Every day we've spent together, I've fallen more and more for her. I was in love with her before. Now it's like I can't function properly without her. I can tell by the darkness outside that it's not dawn yet. From experience, I know there's no point in going back to bed. I strip and don on my running sweats.

I tiptoe out of the house. Outside, I inhale the

heaviness of a day getting ready for rain. I head towards Blossom Ford Point. As I get there, the first rays of sunshine are coming through the horizon. I sit underneath the cherry blossom tree, right in front of the ford, and watch the water gurgle down the river.

I love and hate this place. The peace here settles my mind a little. I pick up a soft, pink petal and stroke it. It reminds me of Ella's smile. I shake my head at how badly I have the hots for her.

I shake my head to rid myself of the sense of guilt I feel towards Kenzie Gallagher the unknown woman - who is my mother - and stare around me at the luscious greenery along the river and mountain in the distance. Mrs. Gallagher said my mother must have wanted me to have a beautiful after life, that's why she chose this wonderful river as a resting place for us. But I often wondered how anyone could bear to hurt a child in such a beautiful place.

Even though Mrs. Gallagher has only ever given me love and seems content, every time I see her I wonder how different her life would be if her husband were still alive.

After a couple of hours, when the sun is hotter on my face, I get up and head home. I'm not good company, but Ella will wonder where I am. I arrive as she's getting out of her room.

"I didn't hear you go out," she says, her face a study in curiosity.

"I went out for a jog."

I shower and dress, then join her in the kitchen. I make short work of my pancakes and eggs.

"Now that term's about to start, I have a lot of work to catch up on," I say and head to the study, leaving her to wash up alone.

I've tried to be my usual self, but I can tell she knows something is up by the curious looks she gave me over breakfast.

I spend most of the day in the study, keeping myself busy. When Ella comes in to tell me it's lunchtime, she's looking so lovely in shorts and an off the shoulder top, that I'm not sure I can trust my ironclad self-control in the mood I'm in so I ask her for sandwiches. She nods but her smile falters. I frown at her back as she leaves the room. It's the first time we're not eating together, so I thought she might actually like to have some alone time.

When she brings in a tray, her usual friendly expression is back on and I'm relieved. By late afternoon, I know I need to take a break when words start blurring in front of me. I move to the small couch in the room and lie down to rest.

Something soft is touching my lips in the lightest of caresses when I come to myself. The scent of strawberries reaches my nostrils and I inhale, my eyes flying open because I recognize the sweet fragrance and can no longer feel that soft caress.

Honey eyes stare at me with a longing as deep and strong as my own. Ella's face is only a couple of inches from mine. My arm snakes out and pulls it towards mine until our lips are touching again. The movement is so natural, as if this is what I was meant to do.

Soft sighing is a beautiful song in the room, but I don't know if it's coming from me or Ella. Her lips taste as wonderful as they did at the church. No, better even.

I move my lips from side to side against hers, the ensuing sensation shooting electricity straight to my cock and just like that, I'm hard and my body demands more.

I angle my head and with my tongue tease the seam of her red lips. Immediately they part and this time, I can tell the sigh is coming from Ella.

She lets me in and caresses my cheeks. Her touch is so strong, so sure and her response so assuredly hot, that even as my tongue duels with hers, one of my hands moves towards her body.

She shifts closer until her top half is lying flush against mine. Her hands move to my head and she stokes my curls.

I trail my fingers across her chest until I find one breast. She arches as if to give me more access when I kneed it softly. I caress the nipple through the thin top and Ella moans. The sound is so sweet I want to hear more of it. I let go of the back of her neck and touch her other breast too, so that I'm caressing both of her nipples. My lips curve as her moans increase.

I've dreamed about caressing Ella's generous breasts for so long. It's better than my imagination.

"Does it feel good?" I ask as I pinch a hard point.

Ella arches her back further and says something.

"What do you want? Tell me!" I can't believe how sandy my voice is. It brooks no argument, but right now my mind is filled with desire and pleasing Ella, I can't make myself speak in a gentler tone.

"Shirt off!" Ella's voice is raspy too. She lifts up and I help her slide the offending garment off. The lacy blue bra framing her cups is so beautiful that I want to touch it, but Ella's unclipped the bra so I help her with that too. She's so beautiful. I reach up and pull her on top of me.

Then we're kissing again. I've wanted to touch her so badly I snake my hand past her chest and the lush brown skin of her belly until my hands come across the button of her shorts. She lifts a bit and I undo it. I slip my hands inside her panties and curve them around her ass, kneading the soft skin.

She glides against my cock, and it rears up towards her.

I focus on her. This is my fantasy - pleasuring her. My hands massage round her voluptuous ass and hips until I'm playing with the patch of hair on her mound. I inch my hand until it finds her clit. I give it a couple of strokes. Slowly, I rub it from side to side. Ella moans then buries her mouth against my neck, sucking the skin there.

I groan. Touching her feels so good, but the added sensation at my throat almost unmans me. I'm so sensitive there. Inhaling deeply, I focus on what I was doing. I want to see Ella come apart in my arms. So I concentrate on the soft noises she's making, use them to guide me.

I slip my middle finger into her wet pussy, even as I rub the heel of my hand against her hard nub.

"August…" her raw murmur is a breath and a demand.

I insert another digit and scissor both fingers then twist, increasing the pace until she's writhing uncontrollably against my hand.

She arches and I pinch her nipple. Ella comes apart, my name a beautiful song around us.

Smiling, I stroke her back as she lies on my chest, as limp as a rag doll.

Yet moments later, her hand slides between us, and when it touches my cock, my smile vanishes.

"I want to give you pleasure too. And I want your skin on mine." She's a little shy, but the truth in her voice is clear. It spreads a warmth in my heart and turns my already hard shaft into steel.

"Aww Ella, let me take my shirt off."

She lets go of me and lifts up. I slide out from underneath her and she turns until she's lying on her back.

I rip my shirt off and throw it aside. Something catches the corner of my eye and I look up into my reflection on the mirror on the opposite side of my desk. Reality comes knocking in.

I take a couple of breaths to steady myself. To bring back my rigid self-control.

"August." Ella's arm reaches up to me.

I swallow. I want to take her hand, lie back down and fuck her until she's so sated, she can't speak.

I shake my head and turn away. I can't do this to Ella. Instead of ravishing her, I should protect her. Even if it's from me. I clear my throat.

"I'm so sorry Ella. That shouldn't have happened. It isn't fair to you."

Then I grab my shirt and march out of there as if the hounds of hell are chasing me. Because staying means taking her soft body and I love Ella too much to let her be involved with a man who's broken and too old for her. The beautiful, strong young woman that she is deserves better.

# 7 ELLA

IT'S THE LAST week of September and I can tell fall is coming. There's a nip in the air during the days and it's much colder in the evenings. I wrap my hands more tightly around the mug of cocoa I've been nursing and, for what feels like the millionth time, try to make myself focus on the notes I took during my first year of college.

It doesn't work. I've been spacing out so much I'm starting to worry about myself. I poke the curtain aside and peer into the darkness outside. The front drive is as quiet as a morgue. August's going to be late again.

Since that day, I've only seen him twice. Even then, I think it was by accident. He's like a spy, who comes in the dead of night, leaves at the crack of dawn and moves silently around the house.

"I'm sorry Ella. You're here under my protection. I shouldn't have done that to you," he'd said both times

I tried to talk to him.

I wanted to scream that he'd given me the best orgasm of my life. But he'd vanished as soon as he said the words.

Meals don't taste the same as they did when I ate with him. The house seems massive and unwelcome, even though I put up pictures of August and me with Mrs. Gallagher and the kids the day we visited the orphanage. The flowers I place in the kitchen and sitting room don't brighten the house as much as they used to.

It's late. After giving up on my notes, I get ready for bed. I lie awake under the covers until I hear August. I rush to the door as silently as I can and inch it open just in time to see his bedroom door close.

I return to bed. When I wake up the next morning, he's gone.

Now that August is working and not eating at home, I spend more time at the orphanage. More and more, I love my time there. I've started helping with the books as well, using the skills I learned my first year at college.

I'm taking a break in the garden, sitting on an old wooden bench when Mrs. Gallagher comes out and throws herself beside me, her short bob of white hair a little messed up. It's been a busy morning even though I loved every minute. Not having a moment to think about the pain in my heart is a blessing.

We watch a frog leap in the pond a few steps away

from us.

"Something has been bothering you," Mrs. Gallagher says.

I smile. Despite her gnarled hands and rickety legs, Mrs. Gallagher's eyes are still as sharp as my mother's. I could hide nothing from her, either. Talking to a friend helps me most times, but I can't talk to my sister about this and Winona's been so busy with her postgraduate studies, I've been mulling over things by myself.

There isn't anyone in Blossom Ford that knows August the way Mrs. Gallagher does, however I don't know how to broach the subject. It's like talking to a mother-in-law about marital problems. Besides, she doesn't know our marriage is a contract.

"Is August not treating you well? It's very clear he's in love with you, but he can be a moody man."

"He's very kind."

Mrs. Gallagher snorts. "Something's wrong." She stares at me, as if she can pull out the answer from my mind.

"I think my age makes him feel overprotective, so he doesn't share a lot with me." I shrug.

Mrs. Gallagher plays with the plain band around her ring finger. "That's how my Kenzie was at the beginning of our marriage." She suddenly cracks up in laughter.

I stare at her. "How did you deal with it?"

"I was only eighteen when I came to Blossom Ford as a mail-order bride. There were nearly twenty years between us, but one look was all it took me to fall in love. From that moment on, Kenzie had no chance. I took the lead."

I laugh with Mrs. Gallagher, some of the stiffness in my heart easing.

I take a couple of days to decide what to do. I know I can't go on like this. August's beautiful house is meant to be shared, but I'm no longer comfortable here. I want him to see me as a woman who loves him. Someone who wants to share his burdens the way he's shared mine. Even if all I can do for him is listen.

There's no doubt he's attracted to me and enjoys my company. It's time for him to decide if what he feels for me is strong enough to overcome whatever's been keeping him away from me.

When he sneaks into his room at one in the morning, I'm waiting for him in the love seat under the window.

He switches the light and drops his bag by the door. His tie comes off next. He looks as sexy as sin, but even from here, I notice the shadows under his eyes. His beard is a little wild, as if he hasn't trimmed it in a while. My fingers itch to touch the smattering of gray hairs there. I need to be in control of my emotions, so I shut down those thoughts just as August notices me.

"What are you doing here?" His voice is curt with surprise and something else – longing. It's there in the way his eyes rove over me before he turns his back and opens the door. "Go to bed."

Before, if he'd spoken to me like that, I would leave, but not today.

"We either talk here or I come to campus. Choose."

He scowls at me, but I stay seated.

A sigh and I know that for now, he's going to listen. He leaves the door wide open and leans on the wall, arms crossed.

"I can't carry on staying here, the way things are between us."

August raises one brow. I stow my hands under me to hide the fear surging at his lack of a better response.

"We're keeping to our bargain quite well." Impartiality coats every cord of his voice.

"I'm not happy, and neither are you. I've driven you away from your home."

"I'm working- "

"That's bullshit!"

August inhales. His arms are steel bars around his body.

I stand up, unable to sit. I walk closer to him. His eyes slide to the open doorway and hurt tightens my chest.

"Do you hate spending time with me that much?" I blink my eyes but can't help the tears in my voice.

Anguish spreads across his face. "You're the best thing in my life."

"Then why drive me away?"

"How can I not?" He pushes his hand through his hair. "I want the best for you."

"That's you."

"The harbinger of death? A man who's too old for you and has so many scars he's terrified of even losing your friendship? Me loving you will forever remain a dream of mine."

Sorrow for August threatens to weaken me, but his last words speed up my heartbeat.

As if realizing what he just admitted, he goes and stands by the door, face away from me.

I close the distance between us, but I don't leave. I'm never leaving. Not after he's admitted he loves me. I plant my feet shoulder length apart, wrap my arms around his back and lean my head on his broad chest. He's as tense as a coiled panther.

"I love you too." I inject every ounce of truth in those four words. Three times, I repeat that tiny sentence. When nothing changes, I say, "I'm a woman who's mothered a stroppy teenager and can take care of herself. I don't want a younger man. All your scars make you August Ford. I'm in love with August Ford."

A choked sound rumbles from his chest. But he doesn't budge.

Neither do I. "Before you single-handed decided not to love me, I was having the happiest time of my life with you. Instead of making us miserable, you can choose to make both of us happy."

I don't know how long we stand like that before his arms inch around me. He stays like that and I think he's breathing the scent on my hair because his head is resting lightly on mine and I can hear his chest rising rhythmically.

My feet are getting uncomfortable when he lifts me up and carries me to the bed. He lays me down gently, gets in beside me and pulls me toward him, my head on his chest.

I lose consciousness. Muted rays of sunshine cast shadows in the room when I wake up. I'm still lying on August's chest. Carefully, I turn my head. He's staring at me.

Heat creeps up my neck. "Have you been watching me sleep?"

"Yes."

I put my head back where it was before I woke up, away from his probing eyes.

His chest rumbles under my cheek.

"Where's the strong woman who successfully dealt with a stroppy teenager?"

"Give me a few minutes," I quip back from my safe position, happy he's teasing me.

He turns my head towards him.

"I love you," August says quietly, looking straight into my eyes. "I'm not always the easiest of people to live with. I might try and sort things out on my own or share more than you can handle, but I'll always love you."

I think about what he's just said. Knowing that he loves me has given me superhuman strength, where he's concerned.

"The more you share with me, the closer I'll be to you. It's when you don't share that it hurts me. I'm the staying kind of person. But if you're being a pain in the ass, I'll tell you." My voice is as quiet as his.

He searches my gaze until he seems to find whatever he's looking for. Ever so gently, he kisses my forehead.

My heart melts. I want him to feel this amazing sensation too, so I slide up his body to kiss his wide forehead too. My thigh touches something soft and hard. August groans, his face twisted into what seems to me like pleasure and pain.

I stop, totally distracted. I reach my hand toward his cock and gently squeeze it. Another groan is strangled out of August.

I smile and move downwards. I unbuckle his belt, remove it, and toss it aside. An urge to see him grows. I open the button and reach inside his black briefs. His cock jerks in my hand. I pull it out, careful not to hurt him.

August's hands tighten against my shoulders.

"That feels so good, honey."

A compliment has never sounded so sweet. I lick my lips, my pussy clenches. I stroke my hand up and down his long, wide length. A spurt across the top catches my attention. Using my free hand, I flick a long fingernail across the slit there, pushing the viscous liquid into the hand sliding up and down, making the glide smother.

"Yes, just like that." His hips lift towards my hands.

I want to sing. To have driven August to this helpless state feels amazing. But after a couple more pumps, he stops me.

"I can't last long."

August shakes his head, even as he is pulling me up. He sits beside me and starts unbuttoning his shirt. "I want to be inside you."

I remove my clothes too.

"You're the most beautiful woman I've ever seen." Need darkens August's eyes as they snake across my body.

Before I can answer him, he's kissing me. We fall onto the wide bed, our limbs tangling.

"I'm ready."

August slides a finger into my slippery folds. I'm so wet, more of my juices run down my thigh.

"Take me now," I say as hard as I can before August nips one on my nipples and I can only moan.

"Say that again."

He nips my other nipple.

"Make me yours," I say after my moan has died.

He pushes into me a little and pauses. I suck in a breath as I feel myself stretching around him.

"Okay?" A stroke down my cheek.

I nod and push up.

He keeps inching and stopping until he's all the way in. I bite his neck. Just like I hoped, he groans and pumps involuntarily into me.

"Tease," he says, the sweat beads on his forehead

making him all the sexier.

When he finally starts moving, his strokes are so powerful, like he can't control himself anymore. I wrap my legs around his ass and meet every single thrust, the tension inside me coiling until I unravel, his name a voiceless sob.

After only a few more thrusts, August groans as he spurts into me, causing me to shudder with more contractions.

"You're mine, Ella Mitchell."

# EPILOGUE - AUGUST

## Four Years Later

I HUNG UP the phone and shake my head at Ella.

"He's not coming?" She asks loudly amid chattering, music and excited kids' screams in our neatly manicured garden.

"The way his voice sounded; I doubt he'll be leaving his house anytime soon."

"You feel sorry for Caleb, don't you?"

"I know what it's like to be distant and different from everyone around you. For a powerful man to be confined to a wheelchair is hell. It's a shame because in college he lit up any party."

"Not being able to walk when it used to be as easy as breathing must be hard," Ella agrees.

"Daddy, I need you," Sophie's chubby hands pull at my leg as strongly as a determined three-year-old can.

Ella laughs. "Careful, you'll drop Daddy."

Sophie scoffs as if Ella's words are silly, her chocolate eyes rolling theatrically. "Mummy, don't you know how strong Daddy is?"

"You're right Poppet. Daddy is superman."

Ella shakes her head, still laughing. I pass Kenzie to her and watch as our little boy wraps his tiny arms around Ella. I can't believe how good I've become at holding a baby with one hand while doing something else with the other.

I pick up Sophie, hoist her onto my shoulders. "Lead the way," I say.

She points towards the party hostess and I head to the back of the garden where my sister-in-law and a small group of preschoolers are running around. My chest is filled with pride and happiness as I pass a few of my colleagues, Mrs. Gallagher, a couple of people from town and two women from Ella's part-time college course.

I turn back, my eyes seeking her out. She's passing Kenzie to Mrs. Gallagher. I smile, even though Ella is not looking at me. Her love, trust and acceptance have helped me to realize that I'm someone that deserves a happy life.

"Daddy, hurry!" The impatience in my little girl's voice reminds me so much of my wife, that I can't help laughing as I do as I am told..

The End

# MARRYING THE BROKEN BOSS

## CURVY BRIDES OF BLOSSOM FORD #2

## 1 TIANA

I RUN AS soon as the bus door opens. I hate being late. My number one rule is Do Not Be Late. Even though I know better, I ask myself why the bus had to be late today of all days when I usually can tell the time by Blossom Ford busses.

A car is coming in the opposite direction, but I figure I have enough time to cross the street. I dash across, avoiding a big puddle of water on the side of the road, but a couple of steps onto the pavement, a cold rush stops me. I glance at my front and side. They are both wet and so is part of my face and hair.

I turn around, but the car is already roaring off in the distance. A string of curses comes out of me before

I can stop it. Now I'm late and messy. Even the image of Mum standing with her hands on her hips, saying she's gonna wash my mouth with soap, doesn't stop the cuss words. I set off again and sigh when I spot the humongous old house with a wrap-around porch.

I push the bell at the large gate, the butterflies that started dancing earlier this morning doing acrobatics with the added worry of my lateness and visual. I don't want my patient to think I'm a rag doll when they meet for the first time. Not patient, I correct myself, client. And a filthy rich one at that. If he takes me on as his physical therapist, he'll be my boss for the foreseeable future.

"Yes?" The voice is terse over the intercom.

"It's Tiana Remington, the physical therapist."

The intercom buzzes, and the gate swings open when I push it. I race up the long drive, fisting my free hand. I worked hard during my training period and the following years at a rehab centre to know I'm very good at what I do. But this is only my second private gig, and the agency warned me to make sure I'm extra professional with Mr. cooper. There's nothing I can do about the tardiness but I have to do something about my appearance.

Near the front door, I whisk out a mirror and peer at my face and head. I get tissues from my bag and dab wet skin and hair, glad my eye liner only ran a little. There's no time to retouch my make-up. The tissue is only leaving white bits on my clothes, so I give up. I say a prayer of thanks that my top is dark blue and my trousers are even darker, then tell myself to stow away my mirror.

"Is checking your make-up when you're late part of the professionalism you mentioned in your resume?"

I gulp, feeling like a kid caught red-handedly shoving a hand into the cookie jar. I stare in the voice's direction and my breath catches. It's been a long time since I've seen such an amazing posture. A chest that makes me think the man at the door of the house must work out daily offsets straight back and square shoulders, even though he's in a wheelchair. He has green eyes, dark brown hair and a beard I want to pet. I realize I'm staring and clear my throat.

"Mr. Cooper?" Where's my usually calm voice?

"Let's get started, shall we?"

Breathe, I tell myself. I am a professional. I'm good at my job. Being turned on by a man's great posture doesn't make me weird. It's normal, cause I'm human. Also, I will not crush on my boss, I recite as I hurriedly close the distance to the door and get in the house just in time to see Mr. Cooper enter a room off the hallway.

I close the door and walk to the room. As I walk in, he doesn't take his eyes off me. Shaping my lips into my most professional smile, which makes the grumpiest of patients smile back, I hold out my hand.

"We've lost enough time. Let's begin."

I just about keep the smile in place and sit in the chair facing him, putting my bag on the floor. He's mad, I get it. I'd be mad too if I'd been as late as I am, but his rudeness is disconcerting.

"If you can't get here in time, why should I have you as my physical therapist?"

I purse my lips to stop the explanation of how I'd actually left extra early to ensure I got here early, but the bus had broken down and the next one had been late too. There was an air about Caleb Cooper that screamed of confidence, strength and self-discipline. He wouldn't care about excuses.

I look at him and make my voice strong. "I want to open a private practice by the time I'm 30. Being financially stable is crucial to me. As you will have heard from the client that recommended me, I know what I'm doing. I'm very discreet and am willing and able to carry out any other housekeeping or administrative tasks you may require. I believe those are the requisites you're looking for. There was an unavoidable circumstance today. I apologize; it won't happen again." Heartbreak over Mum and Dad's rows about money before their bitter divorce taught me the importance of money.

He searches my face for a while, then nods and interlaces his fingers over his knees.

Inside, I do a little dance of gratitude as I take out my tablet and find the files his doctor and previous physical therapist sent. I studied them last night, so I just need to ask a few questions and take down any new information before we come up with a treatment plan that'll work for him.

"What do you think is the biggest challenge to your mobility now?" I ask and discover it's not just his posture I like. He answers my questions and asks his own with knowledge that shows he's done a great deal of research about his spinal cord injury.

# MARRYING THE GRUMPY DIRECTOR

## CURVY BRIDES OF BLOSSOM FORD #3

## 1 ALEX

I KNEW THIS day would come. I'm only surprised by two things. First, that my father let me get to my early forties before laying the foot down and insisting I do my duty to marry well and produce an heir for our conglomerate. Second, that my so-called duty is a vision of the most luscious lips and tempting curves I've ever seen. If she weren't a daughter of a family with the same money-oriented values as mine, I might believe that duty might be sweet.

But Nia is a Weston-Parker. Her ancestor was a founding member of Blossom Ford. Her family's business empire of restaurants may be a little smaller than ours, but it is as classy as their regal blood. She looks like a princess and eats like one. We're having a family pre-marriage dinner at their Michelin Star restaurant in Blossom Ford.

Our eyes meet. Hers large and the darkest brown I've ever seen. She doesn't look away; for a beat, then another, before she puts the tiniest bit of steak into a mouth I'm already having fantasies about.

I ordered a background check on her and read the dossier. But the small picture attached to the small file doesn't do her justice. She is twenty-one; the file should have been larger. Most young people in my circle do drugs, drink heavily or have some other vice.

Nia's file is clean. She spends most of her free time with a friend, hanging at the ice cream parlor, going to the cinema and the occasional night out. But I know how influential families can hide dirt, so I'm not falling for the prim way she's sitting. I'm still a little surprised that on her second college summer break, she interned at one of our hotels and received an excellent evaluation.

"Let's toast the union of our children," my father says and picks up his wineglass. "To the prosperity of both our families. May Nia and Alexander be blessed with many children to carry on our union."

Our parents beam at each other. They arranged this mutually beneficial deal. We get the Weston-Parker's five-star restaurants in our luxurious hotels while they get to have a restaurant in a third of our five-star hotels across the world.

Nia lifts her glass in salute and there's a polite expression on her face, but she says nothing. She's a sacrificial lamb too. At least I've experienced the world, but she's fresh out of college. Even though marriages of conveniences are common in our circles, getting stuck to a man twice her age before having time to experience life fully must irritate the hell out of her.

"Why don't we let Nia and Alexander get to know each other?" Nia's mom says. Her eyes and glossy waves of hair are the only physical traits Nia inherited from her. She's slimmer and has that sophisticated look only mature women of the upper class carry.

Mother is older, but she's also slim and has that same air about her. "Alexander, why don't you take Nia to a bar? Somewhere you can have a pleasant chat." She looks at Nia. "Where's the best place to go, sweetheart?"

Nia glances at me before replying. "O'Connors, Mrs. Livingstone. It's not too far from here."

"Goodness, sweetheart! You're going to be my daughter-in-law. Call me Becky."

Nia smiles. It doesn't reach her eyes. But Mother has already turned to the vintage wine in her glass. I stand up, put my coat on, and watch Nia do the same.

"You're practically married. It's fine if you end up in a hotel room tonight." Nia's dad laughs and the other three parents join him.

"It's great to be young, isn't it?" I hear Father say as we move away from the table.

"Do you mind if we walk? The bar's only ten minutes from here," Nia says.

I shake my head. I don't understand the sudden urge to remove Nia from that room, where I know rude comments are being exchanged. Nia's parents are younger versions of mine, in looks, personality and values. I can image the bawdy conversation going on there. Though she must be used to stuff like that, I wanted to prevent her from hearing those jokes.

I thrust my hands deeper into my pockets. I can't do anything about the way my body reacts to Nia. That's biology. However, I can certainly control these feelings of protectiveness and empathy towards her. I'm not letting a woman into my heart again.

Though it's been thirty years, Mother's words are still as clear as the day she uttered them when I caught her making out with another man in our hotel suite, her bra strap half-way down her arm.

"What Mom and that man were doing is perfectly normal. Dad is doing it with other women. That's how the world is. Now, go back to sleep." She'd pushed me towards my room. I couldn't sleep and put a pillow over my head to escape the noises she and the man were making. What they were doing seemed wrong. I couldn't stop myself from thinking I had a bad Mom.

Years later, I learned what my parents did was a choice, but by then I'd stopped believing my family could be like the happy families in movies. I stopped hoping Mom, as I used to call her when I was little, would come pick me up after school like some of the other moms did. I stopped hoping for Sunday family picnics and got used to eating perfectly healthy meals alone.

Whatever this feeling towards Nia is, I'm stopping it before it takes root. Although Father is the CEO of Livingstone Enterprises, I've taken over most of his work for the foreseeable future while he recuperates from a heart attack. Thousands of employees depend on the success of our hotels and subsidiary companies. That's where my focus should be

We walk quietly along Blossom Ford's Main Street, accompanied by the silvery moon, a gentle fall wind and the occasional shout from passersby exiting buildings. I make myself think about the new hotel we're opening in the West side of Blossom Ford, by the mountains, and focus ahead, away from the sway of Nia's hips.

"I'm sure you have things to do. Let's finish these drinks, then go our separate ways," I say after placing a pink gin and tonic in front of her at a corner table in the modern bar. O'Connors is buzzing with people from all ages and walks of life, enjoying drinks on a Sunday evening.

"I thought we could spend a little time together." She plays with the straw in her glass.

What does she mean? "Is there anything you'd like to know?"

Nia takes a long pull on the straw, her eyes facing

the cup. "Not anything in particular."

"Did you read the marriage contract?" I don't want to listen to complaints about the contents of the contract later.

She sits up straighter. Tears her eyes from the gin and looks at me. "I did."

"Good. Do you want to wait a little before trying out for a baby? That's the only thing we have to decide on."

"What do you think?"

I'm used to people being intimidated by me, especially youthful women. But Nia doesn't cower from me. I like it.

Stop thinking about things like this, I tell myself. I can feel the frown forming on my brow.

"It's better to get it done. Then you can have your freedom." My voice is rougher than usual, but the thought of a little boy or girl wanting a hug from their absentee mom tears at me. No matter what kind of mother Nia turns out to be, I'm going to give my child all the affection in me.

She takes a moment to answer. Then, "I agree. There's a five-year term to fulfill the heir condition, but it's impossible to guarantee pregnancy. The sooner we start, the better."

God, the thought of getting her pregnant is making me hard. I drown the contents of my glass. "Are you ready?" Her glass is only half-empty, so I know I'm being a dick, even as I say the words. But I can't believe those emotionless words are coming from that kissable mouth.

"I'm done."

# OTHER BOOKS BY THE AUTHOR

**CURVY BRIDES OF BLOSSOM FORD SERIES**

MARRYING THE PROTECTIVE PROFESSOR

MARRYING THE BROKEN BOSS

MARRYING THE GRUMPY DIRECTOR

MARRYING THE POSSESSIVE NEIGHBOR

MARRYING THE WIDOWED DOCTOR

MARRYING THE SCARRED SOLDIER

MARRYING THE OBSESSIVE CEO

MARRYING THE BIG MOUNTAIN MAN

**THE O'CONNORS OF BLOSSOM FORD SERIES**

MATCHED TO PATRICK

# ABOUT THE AUTHOR

Iris West writes short and spicy romance about alpha heroes and the women they can't help falling in love with. She loves reading all types of romance books that have a happy ending and is an avid Kdrama fan.

Follow or like her on Facebook, Goodreads.

# FREE BOOK

Would you like a free book? Sign up to my mailing list at https://dl.bookfunnel.com/t191w45ryj to receive a copy of Loving My Fake Husband, a free to subscribers only, Curvy Brides of Blossom Ford Series short story.

# HELP OTHERS FIND THIS BOOK

Thank you for reading Marrying The Protective Professor. If you enjoyed this book, please help others discover it by leaving a review at your favorite online book store.

Many thanks,

Iris xx